For my children with all my love.

Bloomsbury Publishing, London, Oxford, New York, New Delhi and Sydney

First published in Great Britain in 2016 by Bloomsbury Publishing Plc
50 Bedford Square, London WC1B 3DP

This paperback edition first published in 2017

A CIP catalogue record for this book is available from the British Library

ISBN 978 1 4088 7274 1 (PB)
ISBN 978 1 4088 7272 7 (eBook)

1 3 5 7 9 10 8 6 4 2

Printed in China by C & C Offset Printing Co., Ltd., Shenzhen, Guangdong

www.bloomsbury.com
www.debiglioribooks.com

All papers used by Bloomsbury Publishing are natural, recyclable products made
from wood grown in well-managed forests. The manufacturing processes
conform to the environmental regulations of the country of origin

Goodnight World

Debi Gliori

BLOOMSBURY
LONDON OXFORD NEW YORK NEW DELHI SYDNEY

Goodnight planet,
goodnight world.

Peaceful clouds
around Earth curled.

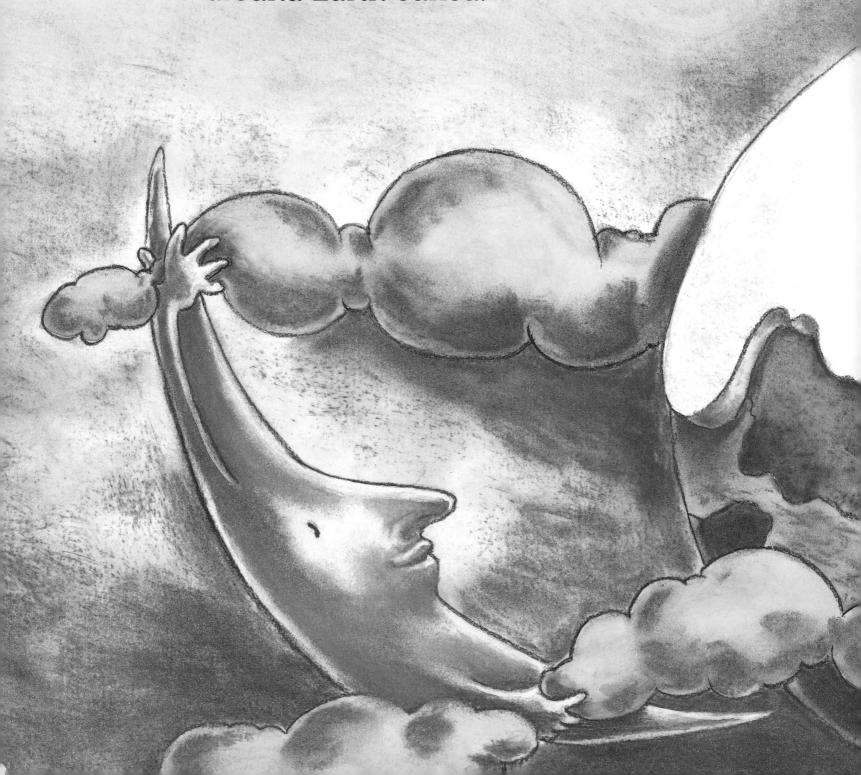

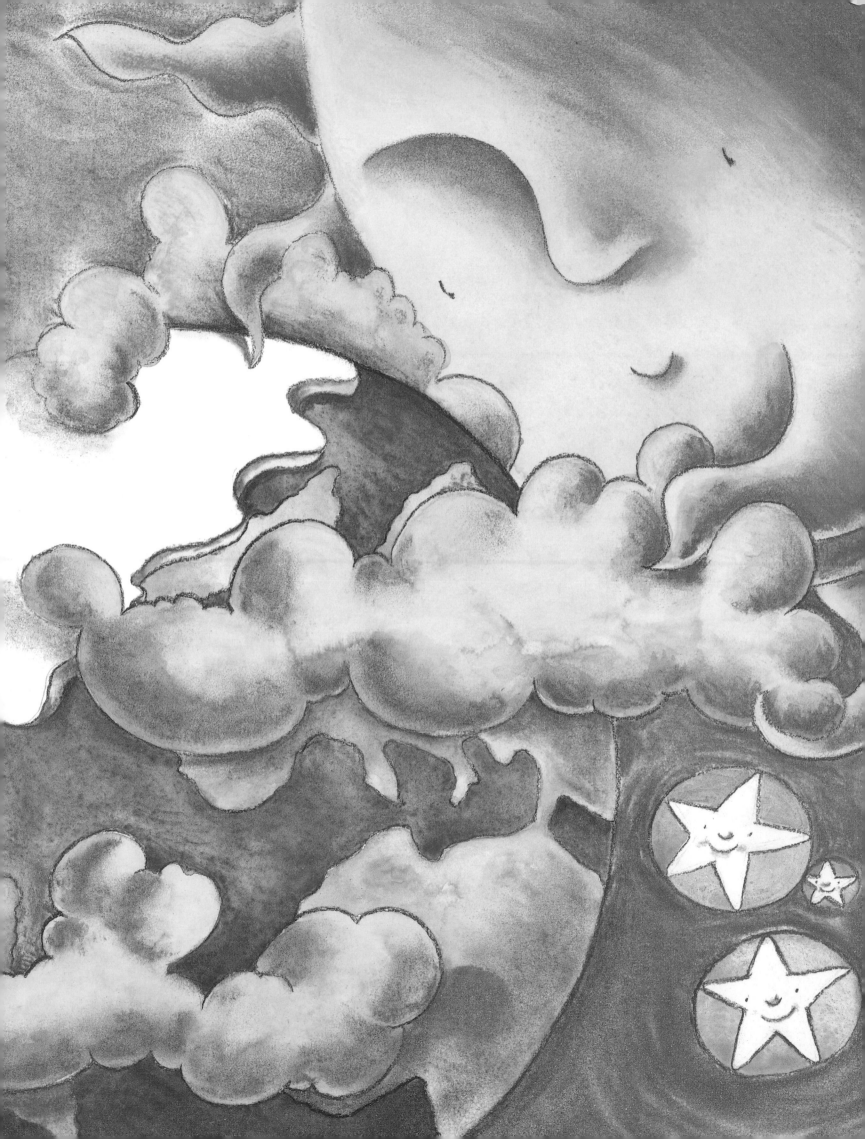

Goodnight ice and
goodnight snow.
Goodnight lights
above, aglow.

Goodnight oceans
deep and wide.

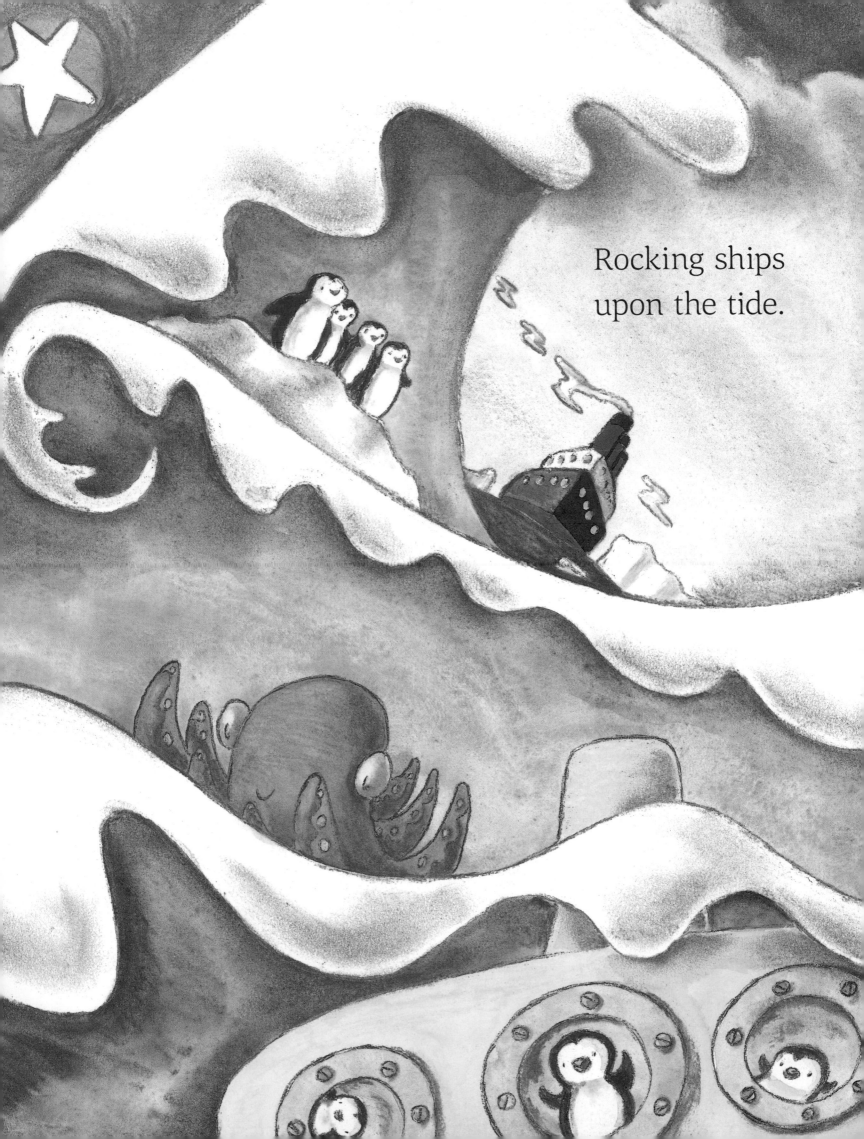

Rocking ships
upon the tide.

Goodnight trucks,
and cars and planes.

Goodnight rockets,
goodnight trains.

Goodnight birds,
goodnight bees.

Goodnight fishes
in the seas.

Goodnight flowers,
goodnight grasses.

Curled up tight
while darkness passes.

Goodnight lions, tigers, too.
And all the animals in the zoo.

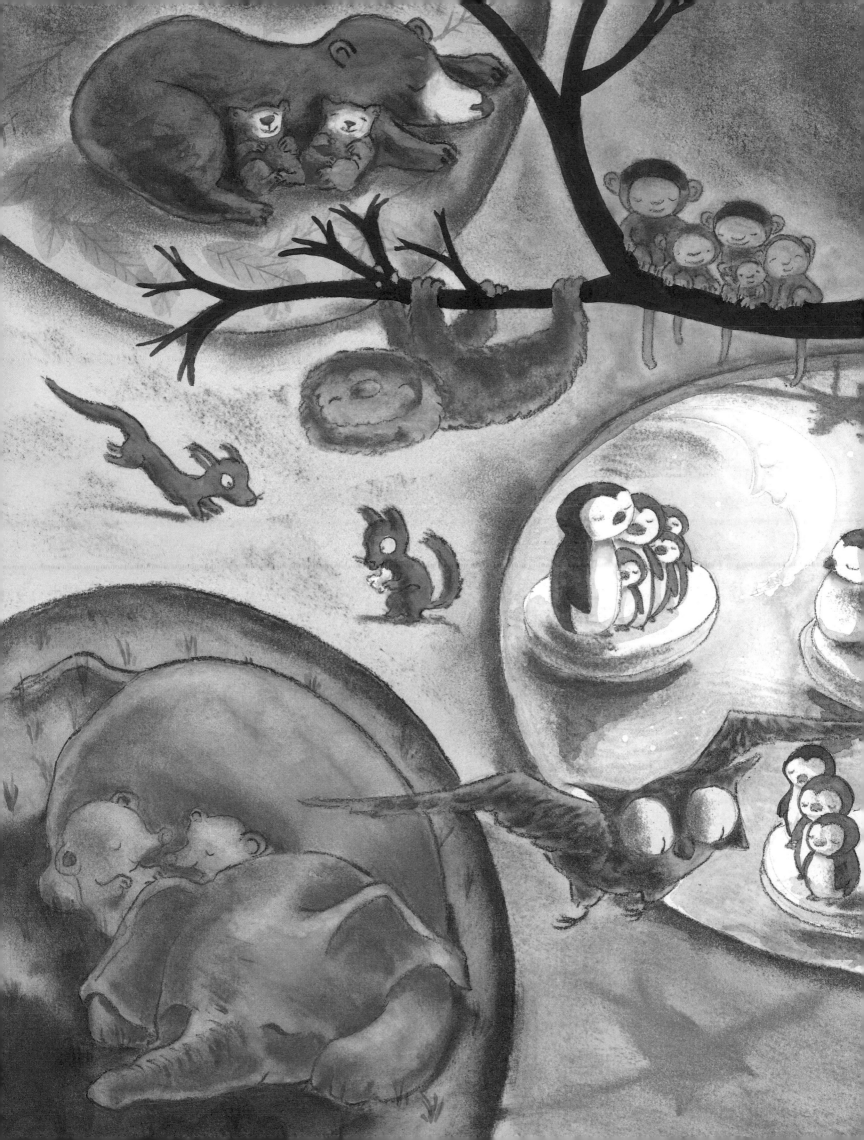

Goodnight shadows
in the park.

Goodnight dog
that doesn't bark.

Goodnight teddies,
goodnight books.
Goodnight sparrows,
starlings, rooks.

Goodnight sounds
of distant cars.
And in the sky,
a million stars.

Goodnight moon,
goodnight sun.
Goodnight, goodnight,
to everyone.

All is well in
my small world.

Around my mother's
heart I'm curled.